Story by Carmel Reilly
Illustrations by Rob Mancini

Contents

Chapter 1

A Present for Mum

On Saturday morning,
Kayla ran into Joe's room.

"It's Mum's birthday tomorrow!"
she said.
"Let's get her a little present."

"But we don't have any money,"
said Joe.

"We can sell some of the apples
from our tree," said Kayla.

After Mum had gone out,
Dad helped Kayla and Joe pick the apples.

Then, he helped them set up a table
outside their house.

Kayla put the apples on the table.
Joe got some paper bags
and put them on the table, too.

Apples for Sale

But the wind was blowing
and some of the paper bags
blew off the table.

As Joe tried to catch the bags,
he bumped the apples.

"Look out!" cried Kayla.

The apples slid across the table.

"It's all right!" said Joe. "I can get them."

Chapter 2

Who Would Like to Buy Some Apples?

The children waited for a long time, but no one went past.

At last, they saw Emma, from next door.

She came running down the road with her little dog, Ruff.

"Hello," she called to Joe and Kayla.

"Hello, Emma," Joe called back. "Would you like to buy some apples?"

Apples for Sale

Ruff barked and pulled on his lead. He pulled the lead from Emma's hand and raced over to the children.

"Ruff!" cried Emma.

Ruff's lead went around the leg of the table.

The table tipped up.
The apples slid across the table and fell onto the ground.

Chapter 3

No, Ruff, No!

Ruff ran after an apple
and bit into it.

"No, Ruff," said Emma,
as she picked him up.

"I'm very sorry," Emma said
to the children.
"Ruff loves to eat apples.
He saw your beautiful apples
and ran over to get one!"

“The apples are from our tree,” said Kayla.

“They look so good,” said Emma. “I would like to buy them all.”

Chapter 4

Help from Emma

Emma ran home to get the money.
When she came back
she had some flowers as well.

"These are from my garden," she said.

“The flowers are beautiful,” said Kayla.

“We can buy Mum a present
and give her these flowers, too,” said Joe.

“She will love them!” said Kayla.